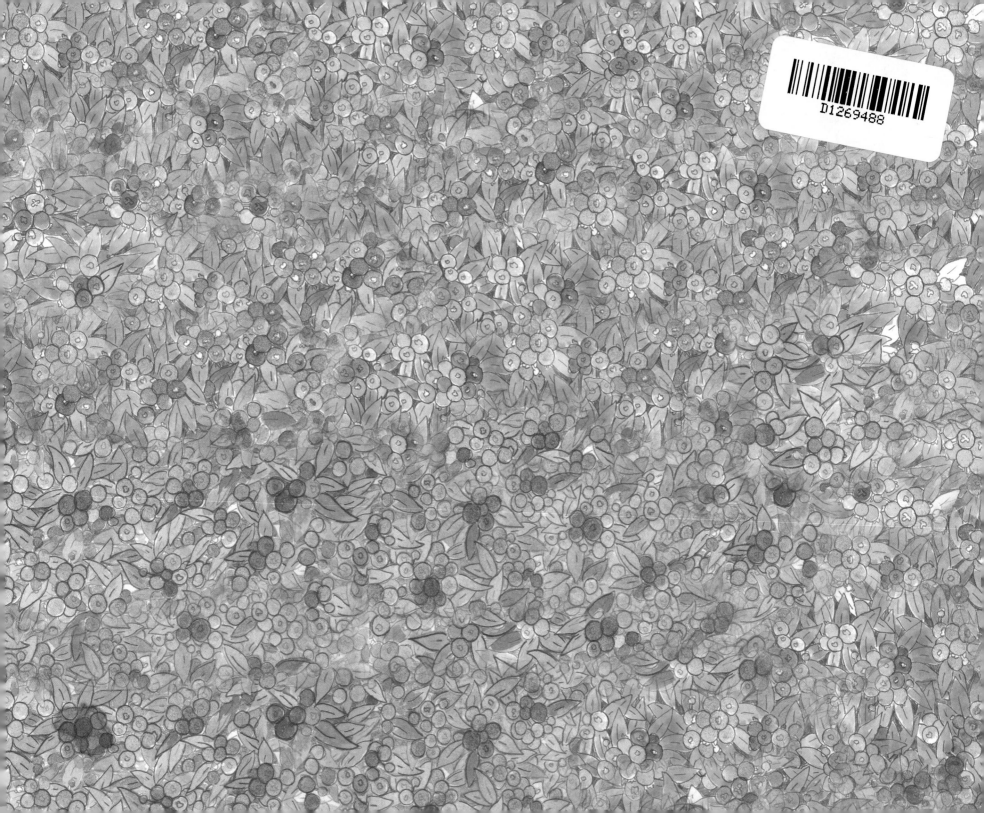

Pentti and the Hungry Polar Bears

By Connie Ahola Loisel and Allyson Loisel

Illustrated by Laura Ahola-Young

Art direction and design by Lisa Wandrei

Published by  AHOLA iNK

Text copyright © 2008 Connie Ahola Loisel and Allyson Loisel

Illustrations copyright © 2008 Laura Ahola-Young

Book and jacket design/layout by Lisa Wandrei.

First U.S. edition 200

Library of Congress Cataloging-in-Publishing Data

Loisel, Connie Ahola and Allyson

Pentti and the Hungry Polar Bears

TXu1-225-018   2008   {Fic}

ISBN 978-0-9816053-0-2
1. Children's stories; 2. Nature; 3. Inspiration

This book was typeset in Goudy Old Style.

The illustrations were done with pencil and watercolor.

Published by: Ahola Ink
                5108 Birch Road
                Minnetonka, MN 55345
                www.AholaInk.com

Printed in Canada.

When one tugs at a single thing in nature, he finds it attached to the rest of the world.

– John Muir –

With shiny new shovels, Pentti and Papa turned over rich dark soil. "This year we'll grow the biggest blueberries in Finland," Pentti beamed. Pentti and Papa cared for tiny seedlings with gentle hands. In no time at all, they had berries – big, bright and blue.

Meanwhile in the icy-cold Arctic, polar bears could not find enough food. Something had changed. Each year brought less and less ice on which they could hunt seals. The bravest of the bears, Ice Bear, followed a sweet scent through the Lapland forests into the Land of the People. There he discovered Pentti and Papa tending sweet blueberries.

"I wonder how berries taste," Ice Bear thought. As he leaned closer, a branch snapped beneath his paws.

Startled, Pentti cried,

"Get out of here Ice Bear!
Go home!"

Ice Bear raced on silent pads through **dark** mysterious woods, across squeaky chunks of slippery ice and frigid waters to his Arctic family. He told them about the people and their bright blue berries.

"How do berries taste?" Ice Bear asked his family.

"Are they chewy like walrus and ringed seal?"

"I hear blue food is poisonous," advised Uncle Bear.

Sister Bear was horrified. "If we eat it," she warned, "our fur turns blue, and then we can't play hide and seek!"

"Stay away

from blueberries if you
know what is good for
you," Grand Polar Bear
commanded.

But Ice Bear could only
think about bright blue berries
and his rumbling belly.

Day after day, Ice Bear returned to study the berries. When Pentti and Papa left one evening, Ice Bear crept closer.

"Will these berries really turn my fur blue?" he wondered.

"Are they really poisonous?"

Ice Bear couldn't resist the sweet smell. He popped the smallest, bluest berry into his mouth.

"Mmmmm," Ice Bear grinned, "sweet, juicy, delicious!"

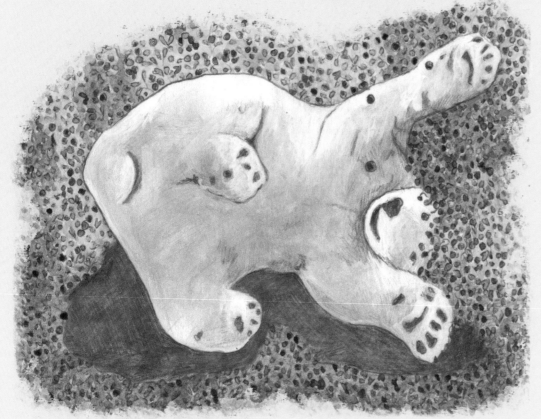

He couldn't stop eating.

"I LOVE berries!" Ice Bear giggled. In no time at all, he filled his belly with berries.

Ice Bear trudged home with a blue chin and a big blueberry tummy ache.

"Berries taste sweet!" Ice Bear moaned. "Nothing like walrus or blubbery seal. I couldn't stop eating!"

"You're going to die!" Brother Bear agonized.

"How could you disobey?" whimpered Mother Bear. "Next you'll be swimming near killer whales!"

"His stomach ache will be a lesson!" Father Bear reassured Mother.

Whispers spread across the Arctic about Ice Bear's discovery.

Late that night, some polar bears dreamed of blue fur. Some dreamed of lurking killer whales. Most dreamed of **bright blue berries.**

Dreams sparked
the bears' imaginations.
One by one,
they paddled through icy seas
following Ice Bear
across Lapland into
the Land of the People
and the sweet,
plump berries.

One by one,
they returned home
with
blue fur.

When Pentti and Papa discovered some of their berries had vanished they shouted, "Someone stole our berries!" They posted signs far and wide.

No one responded.

WHOEVER STOLE
OUR BLUEBERRIES
PLEASE BRING
THEM BACK!
NO QUESTIONS
ASKED

Before long, neighbors complained that many of their berries were missing too. Pentti grew suspicious. He told Papa about fresh paw prints along the forest floor. He told Papa about Ice Bear. "I will spy on Ice Bear," Pentti told Papa.

Late one evening, Pentti sneaked behind a bush and waited.

Within minutes, the countryside was covered with polar bears. Ice Bear and his friends plopped their heavy bottoms in berry patches, ripping tender leaves and crushing sweet berries. Pentti gasped when he witnessed bears swallowing whole plants – roots and all,

while blue juices
dripped
down their
thick, white
fur.

Pentti hurried home. "Polar bears are eating our blueberries!" he cried.

Pentti and Papa rushed from house to house. "Beware of polar bears!" they shouted. "While you sleep, they eat your berries!"

Polar Bear numbers grew. Blueberries disappeared. Anger stretched to all corners of Finland. Finns shook their fists and scowled, "Summers are short. The great Ice Bear must not eat our beloved berries." The people argued and stomped their feet. That day, they forgot how to smile.

Pentti remembered the story of Urho who chased hungry grasshoppers from Finland by waving his pitchfork and chanting Finnish words.

"I will save our blueberries,"

Pentti told Papa. "I promise."

The very next day Pentti confronted Ice Bear. Pentti waved his arms and hollered,

"Mene, jääkarhu, mene!"

which meant, "Go, polar bear, go!"

Ice Bear was not afraid. He swung his sharp-clawed paw and caught the front of Pentti's shirt. *Rrrrrrrrrrr-rip!* Pentti twisted from Ice Bear's grip and fled.

"How am I going to save our blueberries?" Pentti agonized.

"What can one boy do?"

Frustrated, he flopped near the garden where a parade of ants tiptoed past him, lugging a huge rye cracker.

"That's it!" Pentti shouted. "Ants have tremendous power when they work together. People must **work together** to make a difference.

Together we'll devise a plan. Together we'll save our berries!"

In saunas and universities, from quiet countrysides near Vaasa to bustling coffee houses in Helsinki, Finns gathered to discuss solutions.

Erikki and Saara suggested, "We must trap polar bears."

"No," Antti insisted, "bears must be shot!"

"Anything that eats our blueberries must be banished!" Topi declared.

"We sleep under the same sun as the great Ice Bear," Mikko reminded his neighbors. "The same winds blow upon us. We are connected. Let us ask Sun and Wind for assistance."

"Joo! Joo!" the group cheered, which meant "Yes! Yes!"

The following day,

Mikko met with Sun and Wind. "I'll strengthen my sparkly rays to help people," Sun offered.

"I'll direct my mighty gusts to assist polar bears," Wind added.

For days, blazing sunbeams shot across Finland. The ground rumbled as bears plunged into cold streams to escape the heat. Like rolling mountains of white, polar bears crawled over each other. They fled cities. They fled countrysides. They fled saunas and universities. Lured by Wind's cool breeze, they returned to the Arctic.

Papa grinned. "Together we saved our berries!"

"But, Papa," Pentti frowned, "what about Ice Bear?"

"Look," Papa smiled pointing to the sea. "Ice Bear will have plenty!"

Pentti's heart swelled with joy as he watched Wind stretch his arms across the seas, gathering waves that carried fat blubbery seals to the Arctic.

When Wind's cold breath followed, forming more and more ice, Pentti giggled. "Now Ice Bear can hunt again. The bears won't be hungry."

And across Finland, the people smiled once more. It was the Finnish way.

LOPPU
(THE END)

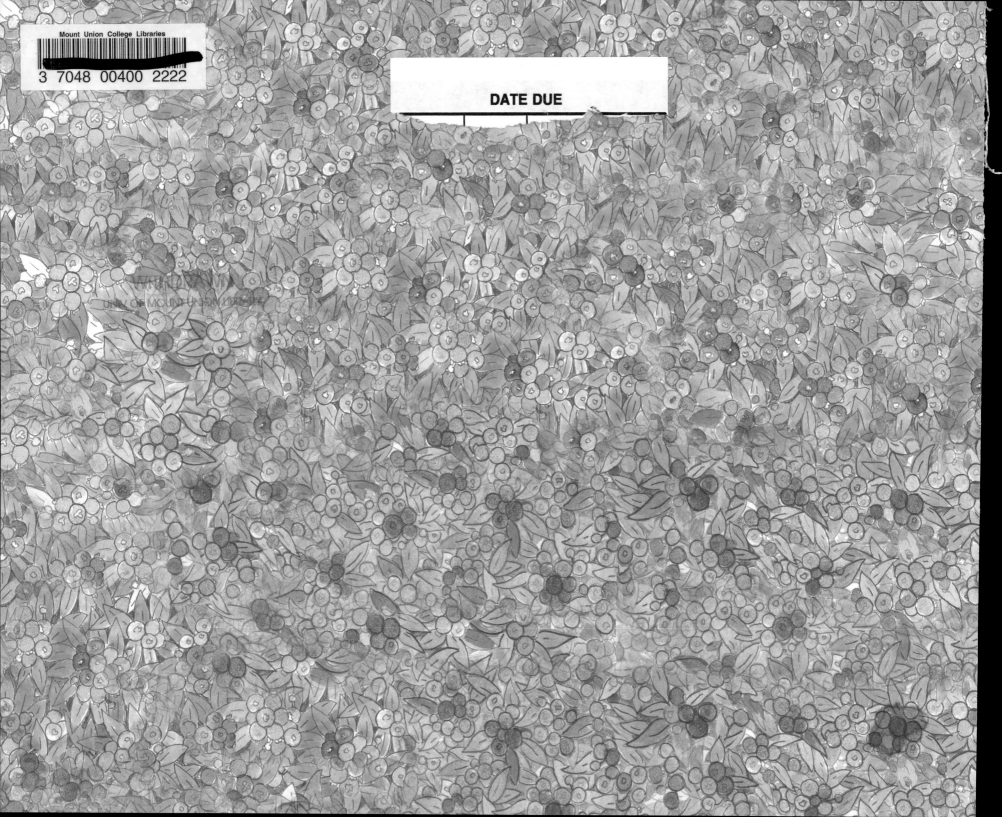

DATE DUE